Friendship Quilt

Written by Cecil Kim

Illustrated by Ha-jin Jeong

Edited by Joy Cowley

big & SMALL

Hank sees Raddie go by.
Her shoulders droop.
Her tail drags.
She is very sad.
Her grandmother died
and Raddie can't stop crying.

Hank is Raddie's best friend.
He knew Raddie's grandmother
and he too misses her smile.
But he is more worried
about Raddie's sadness.

4

Hank tries to make Raddie smile.

He has made her a present.

6

He chats to her and tells her jokes.
Nothing works.
Raddie's hurt is too deep.

Hanks calls his friends together.
He says to them, "What can we do
to make poor Raddie feel better?"

Everyone thinks and thinks.
Then Hank has an idea.

Hank and his friends
get pieces of cloth.
"We will sew them together
to make a quilt," Hank says.

The friends stitch and stitch.
It is hard work.

They get pricked
by their needles,
and their thread
gets tangled.

At last the quilt is done.
The friends take it to Raddie.
"Raddie, this quilt is for you
to tell you how much we love you."

13

One friend says, "This piece of the quilt
is from a blanket I had when I was little.
I snuggled under this blanket."

14

Another friend says, "This piece
is from my favourite dress.
I looked so pretty in it."

"This is from our old curtain,"
two friends say to her.
"We used to hide behind it."

"This is from my baby brother's clothes,"
says another friend. "He is a big pest now
but he was a cute little baby."

A little friend tells Raddie,
"This is a piece of my pillowcase.
I cried in it and I felt better."

Another says, "And this is a piece
of my grandmother's scarf.
It will remind you of your grandmother."

Now it is Hank's turn.

He says to Raddie, "This cloth
is from a skirt my mum used to wear.
My mum and your grandmother
have both passed away,
but we still have happy memories
close to our hearts."

Raddie has tears down her face.
Hank pulls the quilt over her.
"This quilt is full of happy memories,"
he tells her.

One by one, the friends
get under the quilt.
"It's so cozy!" they say.

23

The next day, they are all busy
laughing and eating raspberries.
They are making more happy memories.

Dear Hank,

After my grandmother died,
I felt so hurt and sad.
I don't know how to thank you
for trying to understand.
The quilt you and our friends made
was a heart-warming gift.
You made it from happy memories,
and that made me remember
all the happy times I had
with my grandmother.
Hank, let's make your mother
and my grandmother proud of us.

Your friend,
Raddie

big & SMALL

Original Korean text by Cecil Kim
Illustrations by Ha-jin Jeong
Original Korean edition © Eenbook

This English edition published by big & SMALL
by arrangement with Aram Publishing
English text edited by Joy Cowley
Additional editing by Mary Lindeen
Artwork for this edition produced
in cooperation with Norwood House Press, U.S.A.
English edition © big & SMALL 2015

ISBN: 978-1-925233-88-9

Printed in Korea